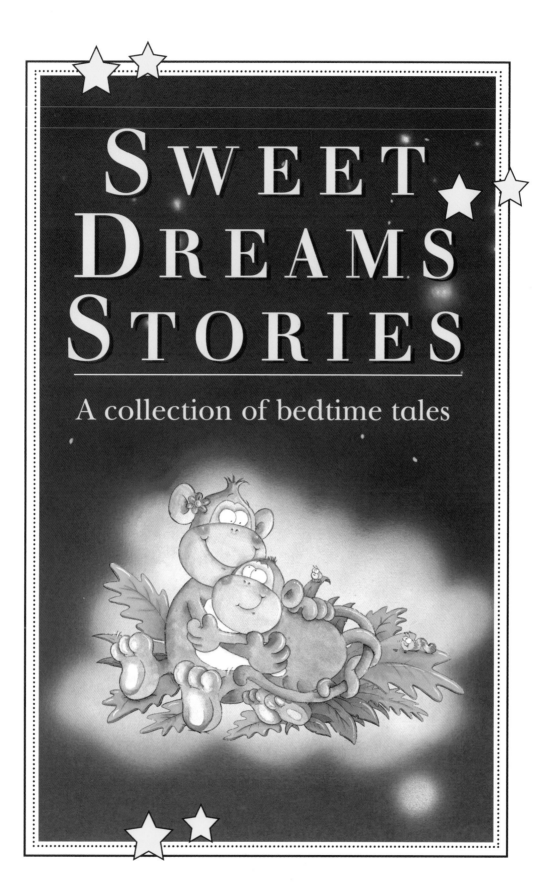

SWEET DREAMS STORIES

A collection of bedtime tales

p

This book
belongs to…

· · · · · · · · · · ·

· · · · · · · · · · ·

CONTENTS

This is a Parragon Publishing Book
This edition published in 2003
Parragon Publishing, Queen Street House,
4 Queen Street, Bath BA1 1HE, UK

Copyright © Parragon 2001

Created and produced by
The Complete Works

ISBN 0-75259-846-5

Printed in China

On my
own

Written by Jillian Harker
Illustrated by Louise Gardner

Deep in the jungle, where only wild things go, Mungo's mom was teaching him what a young monkey needs to know.

"Some things just aren't safe to try alone," she said.

"Why not?" said Mungo crossly. "I'm big enough to do things—

on my own!"

"Now Mungo,"

said Mom, "listen carefully, please. We're going to go through these trees. Stay close to me, and hold my hand. Did you hear what I said?

Do you understand?"

"It's okay, Mom. I won't slip or fall. I can swing across there with no trouble at all," said Mungo. "I'm big enough to do it–

on my own!" And off he swung!

"Hissss,"
hissed Snake,
in a snake sort
of wail.

"That pesky Mungo
pulled my tail!"

And did Mungo hear poor old Snake groan?

No!
Mungo just laughed.
"I told you I could do it
on my own."

"Now, we're going to cross the river using these stones," said Mom. "But, Mungo, I'd rather you didn't do this alone."

"But Mom," said Mungo, and he ran on without stopping, "I'm really good at jumping and hopping. I'm big enough to do it–

on my own!"

And off he sprang!

"That Mungo trampled on my nose!" said Croc.

"Next time, I'll nibble off his toes!"

And did Mungo hear poor old Croc groan?

No! Mungo just smiled. "I told you I could do it on my own."

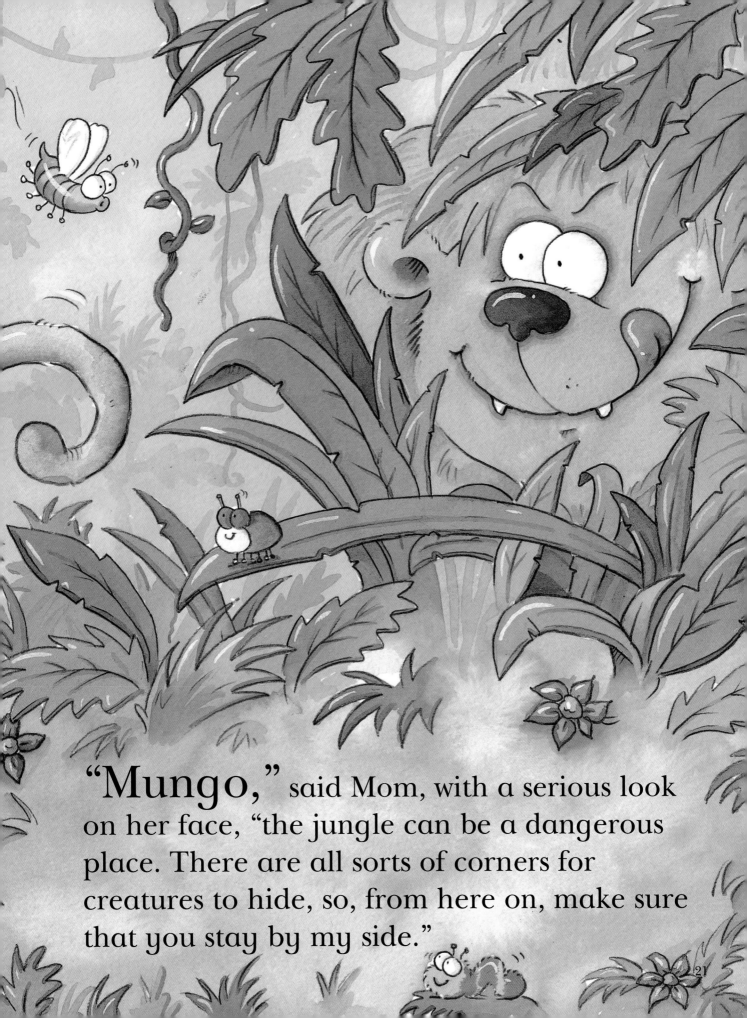

"Mungo," said Mom, with a serious look on her face, "the jungle can be a dangerous place. There are all sorts of corners for creatures to hide, so, from here on, make sure that you stay by my side."

"Oh, Mom," said Mungo, "I don't need to wait for you. I can easily find my own way through. I'm big enough to do it— on my own!"

Lion rubbed the lump on his nose.

"Ouch!

That Mungo's so careless!" he said.

And did Mungo hear poor old Lion groan?
No! Mungo just grinned. "I told you I could do it
on my own."

"I think I've had quite enough for one day," Mom said. "So off you go, little monkey!

Now it really is time for bed!"

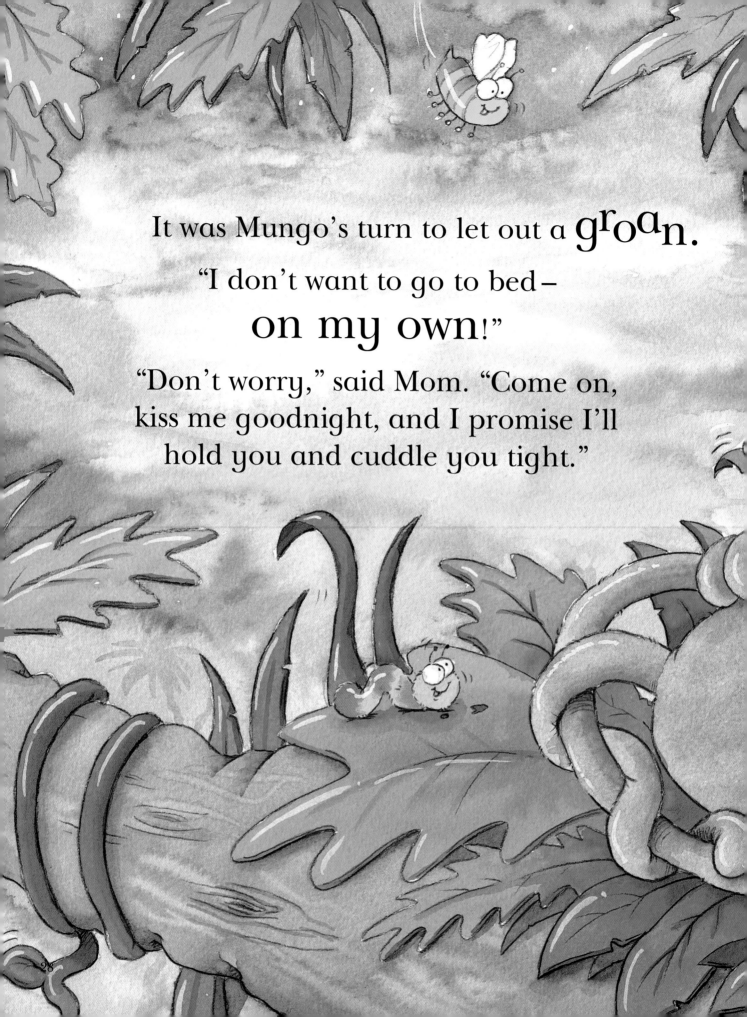

It was Mungo's turn to let out a gr͏oan.

"I don't want to go to bed –
on my own!"

"Don't worry," said Mom. "Come on,
kiss me goodnight, and I promise I'll
hold you and cuddle you tight."

Lion roared, "Is that Mungo still awake?" "Yes!" snapped Crocodile.

"Let's help him go to sleep," hissed Snake.

And into the velvety, starry sky drifted
the sounds of a jungle lullaby.

If you hold my hand

Written by Jillian Harker

Illustrated by Andy Everitt-Stewart

Oakey's mom opened the front door. "Come on, Oakey. Let's go outside and explore."

ROSE
OTTAGE

But Oakey wasn't really sure. He was only small, and the world looked big and scary.

"Only if you promise to
hold my hand," said Oakey.

So Oakey's mom led him down the long lane. Oakey wished he was back at home again!

"This looks like a great place to play. Shall we take a look? What do you say?" asked Oakey's mom.

"Only if you hold my hand," said Oakey.

And Oakey did it!

"Look at me! I can do it!" he cried.

"This slide looks fun. Would you like to try?" asked Oakey's mom.

Oakey looked at the ladder. It **stretched** right up to the sky.

42

"I'm only small," said Oakey. "I don't know if I can climb that high –

unless you hold my hand."

And Oakey did it!

"Wheee! Did you see me?" he cried.

"We'll take a short cut through the wood," said Oakey's mom.

"I'm not sure if we should," said Oakey. "It looks dark in there. Well, I suppose we could—*will you hold my hand?*"

And Oakey did it!

"Boo! I scared you!" he cried.

Deep in the wood, Oakey found a stream, shaded by beautiful tall trees.

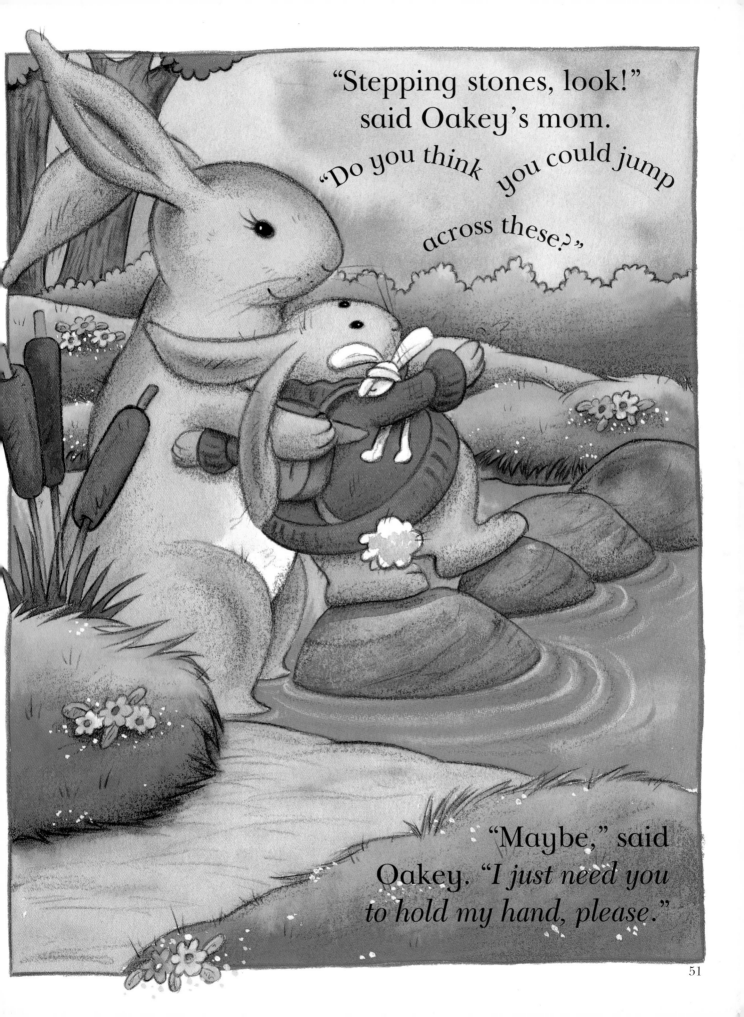

"Stepping stones, look!" said Oakey's mom. "Do you think you could jump across these?"

"Maybe," said Oakey. "I just need you to hold my hand, please."

And Oakey did it!

two...

One...

three...

four...

"Your turn now, Mom," cried Oakey,
holding out his hand.

Beyond the wood, Oakey and his mom ran up the hill, and all the way down to the sea.

"Come on, Oakey," called his mom.

"Would you like to paddle in the sea with me?"

55

But the sea looked **big**, and he was **only** small.

Suddenly, Oakey
knew that didn't
matter at all.
He turned to
his mom and

smiled...

"I can do anything if you hold my hand," he said.

the end

Just
as well, really!

Written by Jillian Harker
Illustrated by Julie Nicholson

Rumpus liked water.

He liked the drippiness and **droppiness,**

the s**plashine**ss and sloppiness of it!

He liked it so much that, whenever there
was water around...

...Rumpus somehow always managed to–

But Mom loved Rumpus, so

every time, she simply sighed—and she mopped up the mess.

Rumpus loved mud.

He loved the way you could plodge in it,

splodge
in it,

slide
in it and

glide
in it!

He loved it so much that, whenever there was mud around…

...Rumpus somehow always managed to —

But Dad loved Rumpus, so

every time, he simply sighed – and
he sponged off the splatters.

Rumpus enjoyed paint.

He liked to
s**platter**
and
dash it,

to spread
and
sp**lash**
it!

He enjoyed it so much that,
whenever there was paint around...

But Rumpus' brother loved him, so

every time, he simply sighed—and he cleaned himself up.

Rumpus liked to find out how things worked.

He loved the prodding and probing,

the **wiggling** and the **jiggling,**
the unscrewing and the undoing!

He loved it so much that, whenever Rumpus was around...

...things didn't work for long!

83

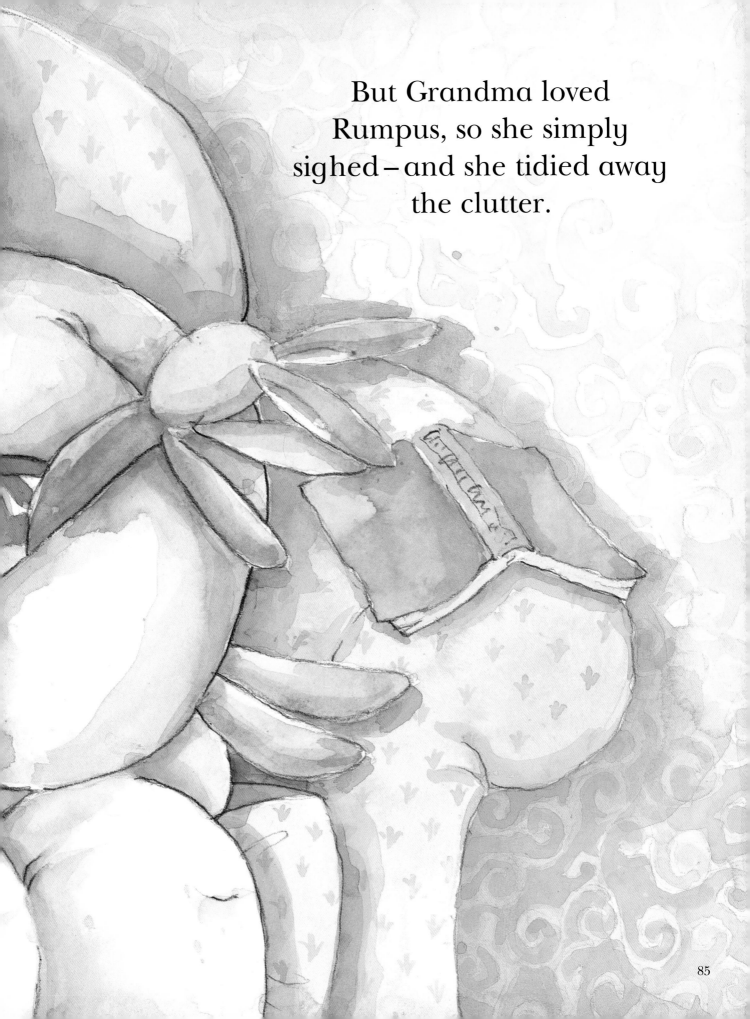

But Grandma loved
Rumpus, so she simply
sighed—and she tidied away
the clutter.

Rumpus loved his
mom, dad...

brother and grandma...

Rumpus's mom, dad, brother and grandma loved Rumpus...

...just as well, really!

the end